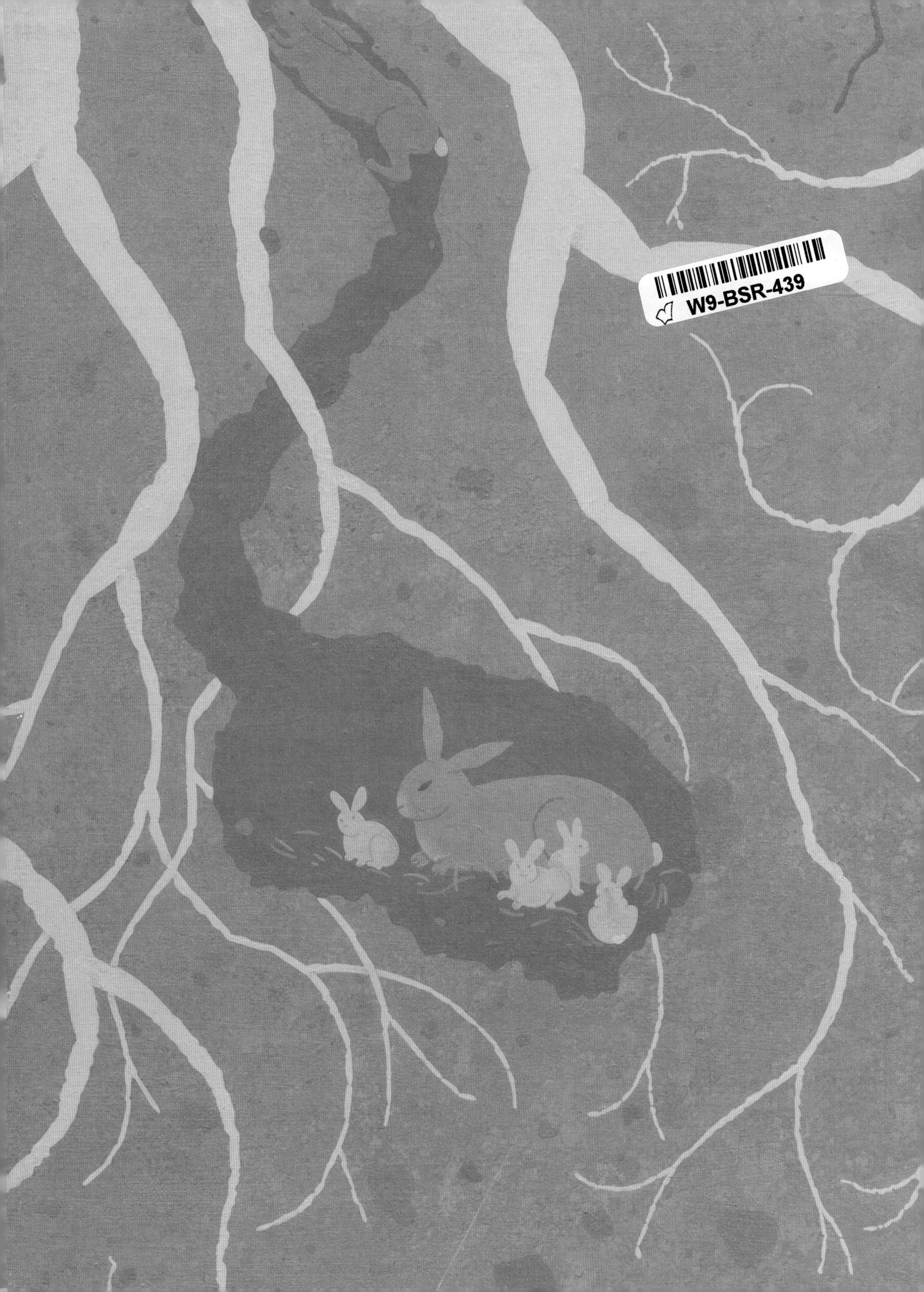

The Man Who Lived in a Hollow Tree

by Anne Shelby *and* Cor Hazelaar

A RICHARD JACKSON BOOK   Atheneum Books for Young Readers   New York London Toronto Sydney

Atheneum Books for Young Readers

An imprint of Simon & Schuster Children's Publishing Division

1230 Avenue of the Americas

New York, New York 10020

Book design by Ann Bobco

The text for this book is set in Regula.

The illustrations for this book are rendered in acrylic on cardboard and linen.

Manufactured in China

First Edition

10 9 8 7 6 5 4 3 2 1

Library of Congress Cataloging-in-Publication Data

Shelby, Anne.

The man who lived in a hollow tree / Anne Shelby ; illustrated by Cor Hazelaar.—1st ed.

p.   cm.

"A Richard Jackson Book."

Summary: Carpenter Harlan Burch, who builds everything from cradle to casket, plants two trees for every one he cuts down, and when he is very old, his sap begins to rise, he grows young again, and starts a family that still lives all over the mountains.

ISBN-13: 978-0-689-86169-7

ISBN-10: 0-689-86169-9

[1. Carpenters—Fiction. 2. Trees—Fiction. 3. Ecology—Fiction. 4. Tall tales.] I. Hazelaar, Cor, ill. II. Title.

PZ7.S54125Man 2009

[E]—dc22   2008010369

For Ace, Leo, and Luke,
running 'round the family tree
—A. S.

For Matt
—C. H.

Way back in the mountains, way back
in time, there once was a man who lived
in the hollow of a sycamore tree.

And lived

and lived

and lived

and lived

and lived.

His name was Harlan Burch, and the trees back then were a lot bigger than they are now.

The whole thing got started because Harlan Burch was a carpenter.

He made tables and chairs, bedsteads and butcher blocks, baskets, bowls, hoe handles, churn dashers, walls, window casings, split rail fences, doors, floors, and gee haw whimmy diddles.

Everything from cradles to coffins was Harlan Burch's motto.

Everything from cradles to coffins

So he spent a lot of time in the woods, noticing things.

And picking out trees to make things from. Pine for this, poplar for that, maple or oak for something else.

And every time he cut one tree, Harlan Burch planted two trees back.

Somebody else might need a tree someday was Harlan Burch's philosophy.

One day he was in the woods, noticing things, and he spied a bird's nest. Then he spied a squirrel's nest, a fox hole, a rabbit hole, and one giant sycamore big enough for a bear to live in.

Or Harlan Burch, thought Harlan Burch. And he stepped inside.

"An ideal residence," Burch declared. And he moved in that very day—lock, stock, and barrel.

There was a sight of work to be done, of course. There always is, when you move into a new place.

But before long he had it all fixed up. Nothing fancy, understand.

But comfortable,

comforting.

Home.

And so Harlan Burch lived in the hollow of a sycamore tree.

And lived

and lived

and lived

and lived

and lived.

He lived to be a very old man. And still he kept right on living. And right on planting trees.

And then an unusual thing happened.

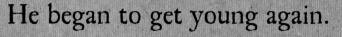

He began to get young again.

uppers and lowers both, hard as hickory nuts.

He grew a whole new set of teeth in his mouth,

His old bald head sprouted all new hair,

thick as leaves on a tree. His old skin peeled off like sycamore bark,

and the new skin underneath was smooth as a baby's bottom

His sap rose.
His limbs got limber, and he took up dancing.

All that dancing just naturally led to courting.
Courting led to marrying.

And marrying led to . . .

A big gang of children running 'round the family tree.

And Harlan Burch kept right on living.

And planting and living . . .

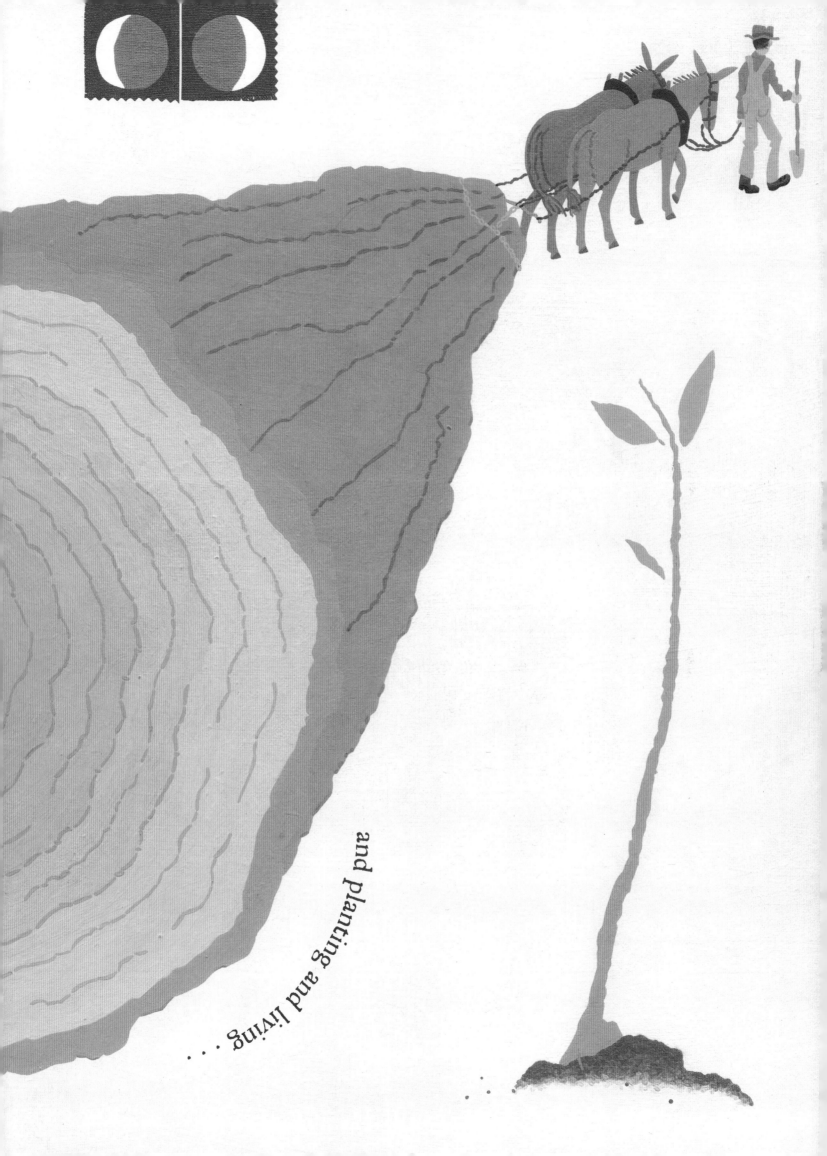

... and planting and living

and living

and living

and living.

Right up to the day he died.
At the grand old age of a hundred and forty-two.

Harlan Burch is gone now. And so is the giant sycamore.

But they've still got kinfolks living

and living

and living

all over these mountains.

From the Illustrator

Working on the illustrations for this book gave me the chance to research the rich, natural, and cultural environment of Appalachia, and I wanted to find ways of incorporating what I had learned about its plants, animals, history, crafts, and traditions into the artwork. The quilt squares emerged as a way to weave in additional information, convey the passing of time, and interact with the main illustrations while referring to the Appalachian tradition of quilting.

Quilting seemed, to me, representative of the social fabric of Appalachia. Quilting bees were a source of joy and an excuse for social gatherings, as well as an opportunity to express creativity. Quilts were frequently created in association with important community events, such as weddings and births—they are storytellers.   – C. H.

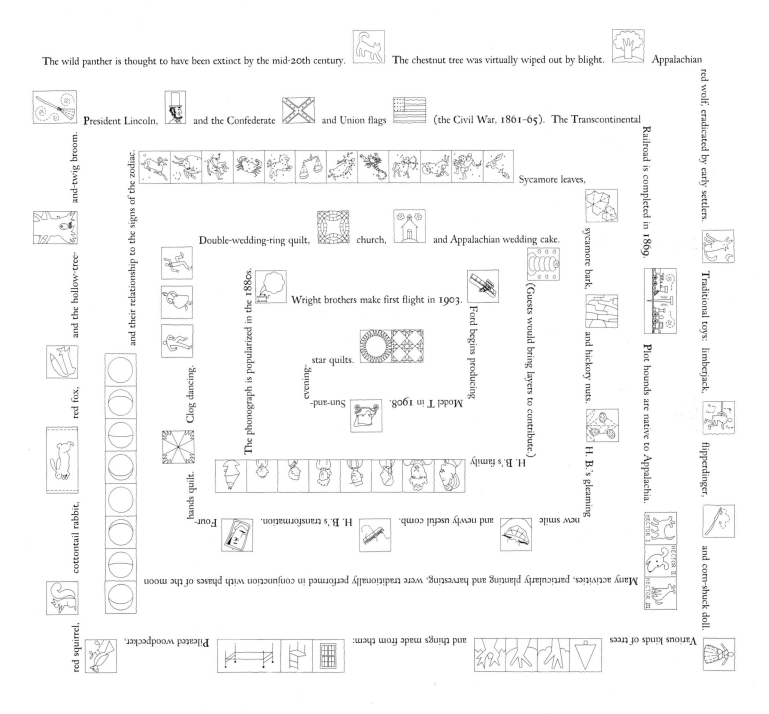

The wild panther is thought to have been extinct by the mid-20th century.   The chestnut tree was virtually wiped out by blight.   Appalachian red wolf, eradicated by early settlers.

President Lincoln, and the Confederate and Union flags (the Civil War, 1861-65). The Transcontinental Railroad is completed in 1869.

Traditional toys: limberjack, flipperdinger, and corn-shuck doll.

and-twig broom.

and the hollow-tree-

red fox,

cottontail rabbit,

red squirrel,

and their relationship to the signs of the zodiac.

Double-wedding-ring quilt, church, and Appalachian wedding cake.

Sycamore leaves, sycamore bark, and hickory nuts. H. B.'s gleaming new smile

Clog dancing.

The phonograph is popularized in the 1880s.

Wright brothers make first flight in 1903.

star quilts.

Sun-and-evening- Model T in 1908.

Ford begins producing

(Guests would bring layers to contribute.)

hands quilt.

Four-

H. B.'s family

H. B.'s transformation. and newly useful comb.

Plot hounds are native to Appalachia.

HECTOR I

HECTOR II

HECTOR III

Many activities, particularly planting and harvesting, were traditionally performed in conjunction with phases of the moon

Pileated woodpecker, and things made from them: Various kinds of trees

From the Author

The Man Who Lived in a Hollow Tree is based on an old story people used to tell in southeastern Kentucky, where I live. It was passed down one branch of my family tree and told to me by my uncle, Millard Bishop. He said there was a man in Harlan County, Kentucky, who lived in a hollow tree and, in old age, grew all new teeth and hair. I added the parts about his being a carpenter, dancing, marrying, and planting trees.   –A. S.